Amica

And the

Magical Fruits

By Stephen Vogel

& Amelia Vogel

Once upon a time, there stood a magical land amid the mighty mountains, and all the animals that lived there, had strange magical powers.

Tie-dyed Tiger loved to eat fruits from the magical Toomara tree. The fruits gave Tie-dyed Tiger magical powers and super strength.

One day, during a very strong snowstorm, Tiger got lost while looking for the Toomara tree. Luckily, he was found by his friend the Rainbow Skunk.

They took shelter in Rainbow Skunk's cave. After some time, they grew hungry, but there was no food left in the cave.

Time passed by and eventually the snowstorm died down, and they could go out of the cave to find food. But, to their disappointment, the snow storm had been so strong that the magical Toomara tree was buried under many feet of snow. They dug, and dug, and dug, but they could not find the tree.

So they decided to move down the mountain to seek food. Along, their way, they met Sparkle Bear. He used to feed from the magical Drampa bush which also was buried by the storm. All he had left was one magical berry from the bush, and he kept it in his bag on his back. He joined Tie-dyed Tiger and Rainbow Skunk down the mountain in search of food.

After a long walk, they reached a forest and hoped they would find food there. The trees and bushes there did not look like their magical trees and, YUCK! The fruits from the trees did not taste like their magical fruits either. They searched, and searched but they did not find any trees like their Toomara or Drampa trees.

After a while, Sparkle Bear and Rainbow Skunk started to groan from hunger. Tie-dyed Tiger assured them that they will find food soon; they just needed to keep looking.

Sparkle Bear decided it was time to share the one magical berry he had brought with him in his bag. He set the berry upon a stump, and they all headed to the nearby stream to clean up.

When they returned, they quickly split the berry three ways and ate it up. The berry was delicious but much too small to satisfy their hunger.

Suddenly, they heard a growl from the trees on the edge of the clearing. Tie-dyed Tiger yelled out asking who was there. And then… a large gray dragon popped out from beyond the trees!   Tiger, Skunk, and Bear scurried back to the edge of the clearing in fear.

The dragon didn't seem to show any anger though. Actually, she seemed sort of sad. Seeing this, Skunk slowly approached the dragon and asked why she was sad. The dragon said that she had seen the bright looking berry on the stump, but they had beaten her to it. She herself was looking for food and had never seen such a fruit in her land.

Tiger explained to her that it was one of the many magical fruits that come from their magical land.

Dragon was very fascinated by the colorful Tie-dyed Tiger and Rainbow Skunk. She was surprised at how Sparkle Bear sparkled so amazingly.

The three visitors explained to her that this was what their kind was like in the magical land up in the mountains.

The Dragon thought it was strange and different, but she also thought they were beautiful and kind and liked them very much.

She told them her name was Amica.

Tiger, Skunk, and Bear explained to her the reason they came down from their magical land. They told her stories about how Tiger and Skunk enjoyed all the different magical fruits that came from the Toomara tree. And how Bear loved the juicy berries off the magical Drampa bush. They told the dragon of how the magical fruits gleamed with many different colors and sizes, and they all tasted amazing. They went on to explain how a large snowstorm covered their home and had hidden their food source.

Amica was fascinated by the stories of the three magical beasts from the unknown magical land. Then she felt saddened at her own appearance. Her gray complexion made her feel less beautiful than the new visitors.

What Amica didn't know though was that Tiger, Skunk, and Bear were actually admiring her. They had never seen such a magnificent creature and thought she was wonderful.

Bear told Amica that her wings were marvelous, and he loved how they stretched out from her back.

Skunk was amazed by the dragon's scales and told Amica that it reminded her of the beautiful fish that swam in the pond near her cave.

Tiger was especially impressed by Dragon's tail, as it was long and had a gorgeous mane at the end that flowed in the breeze like waves of the ocean.

Amica was pleased to hear such nice things about her and was happy that they didn't see her as strange.

Amica was saddened again when she remembered that her new friends had lost their food and were hungry from the long trek down the mountain. She told them that she would help them find food.

Tiger, Skunk, and Bear were very glad that the dragon was willing to help them since she knew the land. So Amica led them on their way to show them many places around the forest where she used to find food.

Along their way, they came across a creek, and there was no way for the three magical creatures to cross over, because none of them could swim.

Since Amica could fly, she knew she could fly over with her wings, and was just about to offer to carry her friends across, but before she could, Skunk shot a bright rainbow bridge over the creek with her tail!

They all crossed over safely. Once they got to the other side, they noticed that Skunk had lost most of her color and was looking grayish. Skunk said she was also feeling weak.

Tiger knew what was happening. He said it was the magical fruits from their land that kept them strong and magical. And now, without them, Tiger, Bear, and Skunk were starting to lose their strength.

Amica was very eager to help her friends find the magical fruits fast. She brought them to the beautiful orchard near the waterfall. The three were amazed by its beauty.

The mist from the waterfall fell over the fruits on the trees and gave them a sparkle that almost made them look magical themselves. Amica said they were called 'apples', and though they weren't really magical, they were very tasty and maybe they would help.

Bear's stomach growled, and he couldn't wait to try this new fruit. But, the apples were very high in the tree and the three magical creatures could not reach them.

Amica knew she could help; with her long neck, she could easily reach the apples. But again, before she could offer, Tiger sprang high in the air with a magical force that left a colorful tie-dye trail behind him. He flew high into the tree and grabbed many apples and brought them back down to his friends. Not long after he landed, like Skunk, he too lost his color and became weak.

Amica quickly urged them to eat the apples. The three each ate an apple and though tasty, they did not bring their color back and seemed to upset their stomachs since they were not used to this kind of fruit.

Amica began to feel like she wasn't being very useful to her friends. Then she remembered a spot that had some other kind of fruits that she was sure would work. So she led the way, and they followed.

As they neared the spot Amica was leading them to, it started to get dark. Amica was concerned that they would not be able to see the berries on the bushes in the dark. Then she remembered that the fire from her breath could light up the area, so they could see.

Just as she took a deep breath to make a flame, she was stopped by an immense light that brightened the whole area. Sparkle Bear's magical fur was lighting up the entire area with dazzling lights. The light frightened the fireflies in the bushes, and they fluttered all around. Their flashing lights added even more glamour to Bear's sparkly light show.

Bear and the others were now able to see the bushes with the berries on them. Bear was very excited as the bushes reminded him of his magical Drampa bushes back home.

Amica once again urged Tiger, Skunk, and Bear to eat. The three tried the little red berries and enjoyed the flavor much, but again they seemed to upset their stomachs and did not restore Tiger's and Skunk's magic and strength.

In fact, Bear lost his magic sparkle as well and his magnificent light faded away.

So now, Tie-dyed Tiger no longer had his Tie-dye, Rainbow Skunk no longer had her Rainbow, and Sparkle Bear no longer had his sparkle.

Amica felt very sad that she was not able to help her friends find food that would help them. They were very weak now as they had used up the rest of their magic when she could have helped. They were all tired at this point and decided they would get some sleep and search for food again the next day.

When Amica woke up the next morning, her friends were still asleep. It was a chilly morning, so Amica decided she would make a fire to keep her friends warm. She gathered some wood and placed it in a pile. She then took a deep breath and shot a burst of fire onto the wood to make it burn.

Tiger, Skunk, and Bear had just woken up, and they saw Amica do this. They were amazed and told her it was awesome that she could breathe fire from her mouth. Amica blushed and told them that was just what dragons do.

Suddenly, Amica perked up with a bright idea! She quickly told her friends to climb up on her back.

Tiger, Skunk, and Bear looked at each other with surprise.

Amica asked them to trust her. So with the little energy they had left, the three, slowly climbed up onto Amica's back. Once they were on board, Amica spread her wings wide and started to flap them. It took a lot of effort with her friends riding on her, but soon they began to lift into the air.

Amica soared high into the sky and headed toward the direction of the magical land in the mountains. Her three friends giggled as Amica flew up and down through the breeze. Skunk asked Amica what they were doing, and Amica said they will see once they get there.

Soon they came over the magical mountains, and Tiger pointed out to where their home was. Amica glided down into the valley where the snow was still covering the area. As they landed, all the magical creatures from the land circled around to investigate the strange new creature that had come to their land. They too were losing their color from the lack of food.

Tiger was pleased to be back but was confused as to why their dragon friend had brought them back as they could not get to their food because of the snow.

Amica told Tiger that she can help. She asked Tiger to tell everyone to move back.

Once all the magical creatures were safely out of the way, Amica stood tall and braced her legs. She took the biggest breath she had ever taken and then released. An enormous flame of brilliant colors of oranges, yellows, reds, and blues swirled and danced out of Amica's mouth. Everyone looked on in amazement as Amica swung her head left and right and all around over the snow. She did this all around the magical land and soon all the snow melted away.

Once again, the Toomara trees, Drampa bushes, and all the other magical fruit trees sparkled across the landscape.

Everyone cheered and feasted on the delights.

After a little while, all the magical creature's colors returned, and they were happier than ever.

Amica was a hero.

Tiger, Skunk, and Bear were proud that they had run into such a great friend. They thanked Amica for her help. Amica felt great that she had helped her friends and others in their time of need.

Tiger, Skunk, and Bear asked Amica to stay with them in the magical land.

But Amica realized she could use her special skills to help others and wanted to travel across the lands to help those in need, but she promised she would visit often.

So with that, the dragon spread her wings and soared into the sky with a smile on her face and a new sense of adventure.

END

Made in the USA
Columbia, SC
30 December 2022

74827556R00020